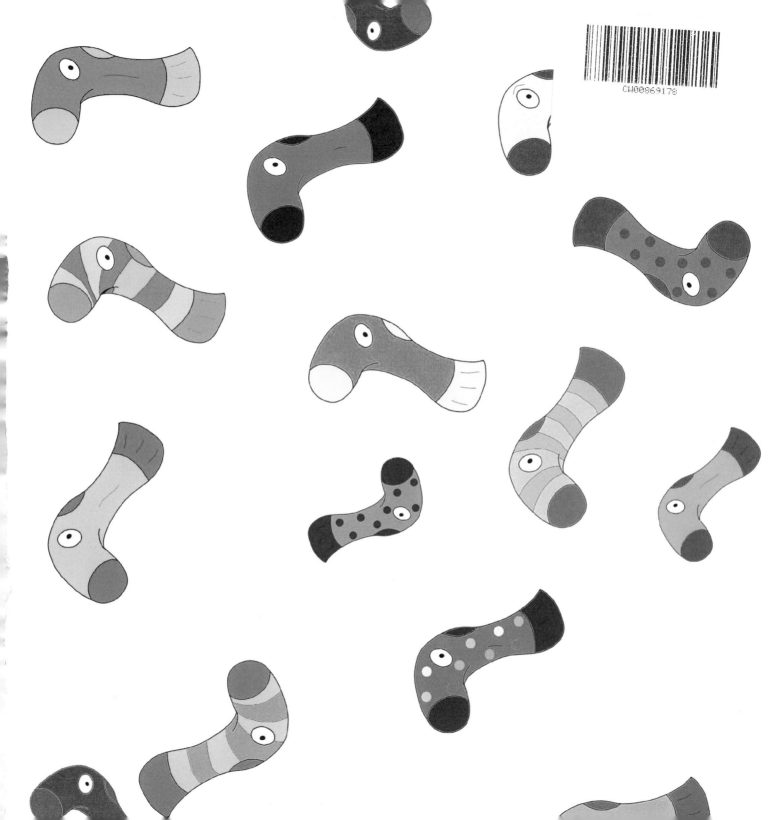

To Mary,
Whom my socks always eluded

First published 2018 by SmileyBooks
Printed by Lightning Source
Copyright © 2018 Niall Cunniffe

ISBN 9781916458505 (paperback)
ISBN 9781916458512 (eBook)

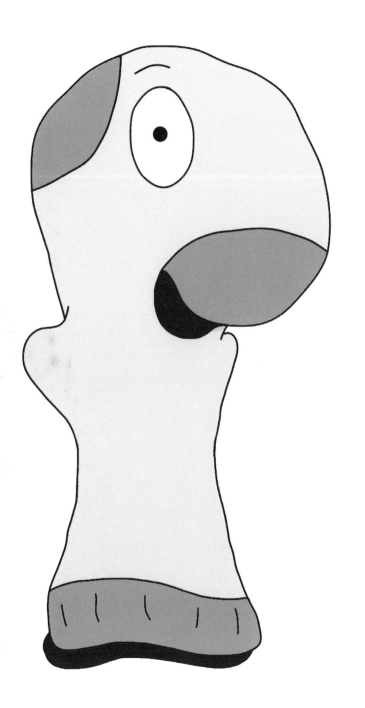

Scott
and the
Runaway
Sock

Story and Illustrations by
Niall Cunniffe

Scott was a little blue sock who lived in a very dark drawer.
Scott didn't mind the drawer, as he had his matching sock Stitch to play with.
One day, Stitch had an idea.

"Scott, we've been stuck in this drawer for far too long," Stitch said. "Let's go explore."

Scott was a little concerned—he'd never been outside the drawer before and had only heard terrible things from the other socks:

giants,

dogs,

and big machines that socks never
returned from the same.

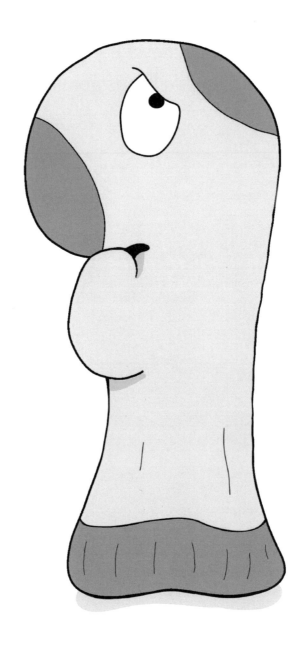

"I'm not sure, Stitch," Scott said. "It's a big world out there."

Suddenly the drawer was pulled open and
all the socks tumbled over each other.

"It's George the Unclever!" they screamed.

George their owner was indeed very unclever,

as he could never keep pairs of socks together.

George grabbed one sock before scooping up another, squeezing them tight as the others ran for cover. That's when Scott saw Stitch, sneaking to the front of the drawer.

"Stitch!" Scott cried.

But it was too late—Stitch had leapt out!
Scott scuttled after him and jumped as high as he could,
just before George slammed the drawer shut.

"That was close," said Scott, picking himself up off the floor.
George was gone, and Stitch was nowhere to be seen.

"Stitch?" he called,
but there was no answer.

He rolled along the floor
and peeped out the door.
Before him was a set of
scarily steep stairs.

"WOOF-WOOF!"

It was Scraggy. Scraggy the dog was the meanest of all,
as he liked to make holes in socks with his paw.

Scott had nowhere to hide. Scraggy ran towards him,
his tail wagging from side to side. Quickly, Scott rolled down the stairs.
But it was too late —Scraggy was right behind him!

Scott ducked and Scraggy went flying, heading straight for the . . .

. . . CRASH!

Scraggy had hit the wall!

"Scott!" came a cry.

Scott spotted Stitch, stuck inside a green basket
next to a big square machine.

Scott had never sprung so fast,
but someone larger than George had just walked past.

"Hurry!" Stitch shouted, as a giant man approached.

Scott leapt on top of the basket and stretched as far as he could.
He grabbed Stitch, only to find his little guitar stuck.

"Pull!" Scott shouted.

The two socks pulled with all their power.
The guitar came free and they jumped with glee,
just before a hand reached in and grabbed all the other clothes.

They hid behind the machine, out of harm's way.
The giant man left while Scraggy snored away.

"Thank you," said Stitch, hugging Scott. "You saved me."

"I couldn't leave my Stitch," said Scott.
"Now let's go back to the drawer."

"Good idea," said Stitch.
"I think I've had enough exploring for one day."

So they returned to the drawer, happier than ever.
And as good socks should, they promised to stick together.

Lightning Source UK Ltd.
Milton Keynes UK
UKRC02n1057071018
330033UK00006B/27